A King for BRASS COBWEB

Dawn L. Watkins

Illustrated By Holly Hannon

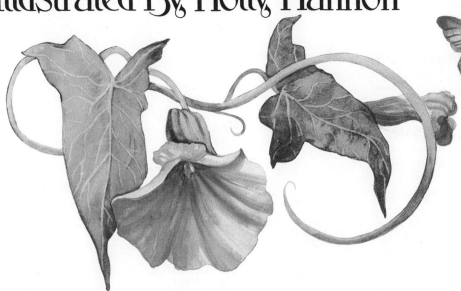

Library of Congress Cataloging-in-Publication Data

Watkins, Dawn L.
   A king for brass cobweb / by Dawn L. Watkins
   Summary: Entrusted by the other inhabitants o⸍
find them a leader who is brave, wise, and true
among distant communities of animals and finc⸍
virtue in both them and himself.
   ISBN 0-89084-505-0
   [1. Chipmunks—Fiction. 2. Animals—Fiction.] I. Title.
PZ7.W268Ki   1990
[E]—dc20

                                            89-275585
                                              CIP
                                               AC

A King for Brass Cobweb

Edited by Anne Smith

©1990 Bob Jones University Press
Greenville, South Carolina 29614

Printed in the United States of America.

ISBN 0-89084-505-0

20 19 18 17 16 15 14 13 12 11 10 9 8 7 6

for Alison Jayne and Tiffany
DLW

for Sally Dorrill
HEH

1 The Beginning

The Kingdom of Brass Cobweb had many wonderful things.

It had purple grass in the Dale of Snails.

It had a pink mist over Mint Lake every morning.

The clear water of Mint Lake tasted like cold peppermint tea.

The kingdom also had a wonderful gate.

It was a giant, shining cobweb of brass.

It had stood at the end of the little valley

as long as anyone could remember.

But the Kingdom of Brass Cobweb had no king.

On the bank of Glass Pond sat Crab, Ant, Rat, Chipmunk, and Grandmother Cricket, talking.

The sand on the bank was blue.

If the wind blew from the east, the sand turned green.

If the wind came from the west, the sand was blue again.

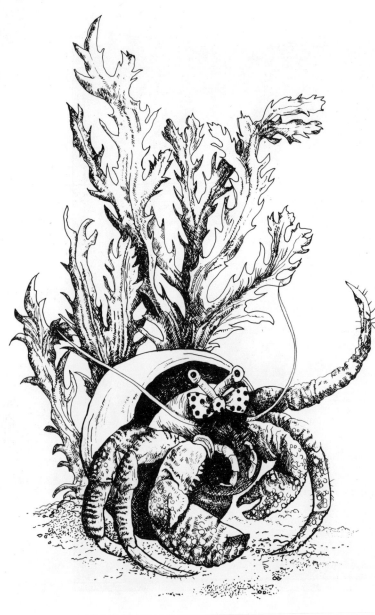

"We must have a king," said Crab.
He sat at the brink of Glass Pond.

"A king?" asked Rat, the banker.

"A king?" asked Ant, the storekeeper.

"A king?" asked Bass from the center of Glass Pond.

"A king!" said Crab, not a bit put off.
He clicked his claw.

"What do we need with a king?" said Bass.

"This can't be the Kingdom of Brass Cobweb
without a king!" said Crab, rather loudly.

"What a crank," said Bass, blinking at Crab.

"Yes," said Rat. "Crab's right. A kingdom
must have a king."

Grandmother Cricket said, "Click."

"Maybe you're right," said Ant to Crab.

Grandmother Cricket said, "Click.
A king might tax us."

"Tisk," said Rat. "The taxes might be high. Then we'll have to sell our property. We may even have to sell the great brass gate to pay the taxes." Rat did not like to spend money.

"Then," said Chipmunk in a quiet way, "we'd have a king, but we wouldn't have a kingdom." Chipmunk sighed at that.

Grandmother Cricket nodded at Chipmunk. "Click," said she.

Bass swam near. He said, "Let's search for a king. Let's give him a chance. We'll let him run Glass Pond and Duck Dock. We'll see then how the taxes will be."

"Yes," said Rat. "If the taxes are high, we'll not have the king. If they aren't, we'll make him king of Brass Cobweb."

"Yes," said Crab.

"Yes," said Ant.

"Yes," said Bass.

They all were quiet then.
The wind skimmed the tufted grass.

Ant said, "We've never had a king.
We don't know what a king should be.
How will we know who to look for?"

Crab said, "Grandmother Cricket can tell us.
She knows many things."

Grandmother Cricket was the wisest in Brass Cobweb. She had read many books and had traveled to many places. She understood how things change and how things stay the same.

"Grandmother Cricket," said Ant,
"what should a king look like?"

"Click," she said. "He may look like anyone. It doesn't matter how he looks."

"Should he not be tall?" said Rat. Rat stood up tall.

"It doesn't matter," said Grandmother Cricket. She got up and limped to the top of the bank. She had a pine-needle cane. She sat on a clover. "That's better," she said with a sigh.

"Shouldn't a king be old like you?" said Ant to Grandmother Cricket.

"Click," said Grandmother Cricket. "It doesn't matter."

"What *does* matter?" asked Bass.

"The king," said Grandmother Cricket, "must be brave. He must be wise. He must be true."

"We will have to go far to find such a king," said Rat.

"Yes," said Crab.

"Yes," said Ant.

"Yes," said Bass. "Who can we send to look for this brave, wise, true king?" He wiggled his tail and fins to keep near the bank.

Ant said, "Grandmother Cricket would pick the best king."

"Grandmother Cricket can't make such a trip," said Rat.

"What about Crab?" said Bass. "He wanted a king first. Let's send him."

Crab lifted himself up on his claws. "The one who goes will have to go far. I have to stay by the water."

Bass swam back to the center of the pond. "I must stay *in* the water. Don't look at *me*."

Grandmother Cricket stood up slowly. "I think we should send Chipmunk," she said.

"Chipmunk?" said Rat.

"Chipmunk?" said Crab.

"Why Chipmunk?" asked Bass.

Grandmother Cricket said, "Chipmunk isn't old like me. He isn't small like Ant. He doesn't need to stay by the water. And he doesn't think of himself. He should go for us." She tapped her pine-needle cane.

"Yes! Send Chipmunk," said Bass.

"Yes! Send Chipmunk," said Crab.

"Yes! Send Chipmunk," said Ant.

"Shouldn't I go with him?" asked Rat. "I am older. I am a banker. I can help."

"No," said Grandmother Cricket. "Chipmunk is able to find us a king by himself. He will find us a king who is brave and wise and true."

"Well," said Rat. "What do you say, Chipmunk? Will you go?"

7

"I will," said Chipmunk, jumping up.
"I'll try to find us a good king."

"Good," said Grandmother Cricket.

"Good," said Bass.

"Good," said Crab.

Rat said, "Find us a king
who is brave and wise and true, Chipmunk."

Chipmunk said, "Ant, will you tend my mill
on Windmill Hill?"

"I will," said Ant.

And away Chipmunk went in a wink
to pack for his trip.

The next day, Chipmunk stood under the great brass
gate. He had a bundle over his shoulder.
He had nuts and corn wrapped in a grape leaf.
The leaf was tied with a corn silk.
He wore a walnut shell for a hat.

"How far should I go?" he asked.

Grandmother Cricket said, "Go as far as Seven Copper Hills. Or go as far as a month will take you. Then come back, with or without a king."

"I will," said Chipmunk. "Farewell."

Rat said, "Take care."

Ant said, "Come home soon."

Crab said, "Bass says to bid you well. I wish you well myself."

Grandmother Cricket said, "Remember, Chipmunk. Find us a king who is brave and wise and true."

"I'll remember," said Chipmunk. He picked up his bundle and went out through the great brass cobweb.

The others waved him off until they could see him no more.

Wits and Wings

Chipmunk walked along Hemlock Highway.

He saw wide meadows full of woolly sheep.

He saw mines with violet stones and chunks of gold.

He saw a glen deep with blue snow.

On the fifth day he came to a thick woods.

The yellow trees swayed in an easy breeze.

From inside he heard a low hoot.

"Hoot," it went. "Hoot."

"Who is there?" asked Chipmunk.

"Hoot."

"I say," said Chipmunk, "who is there?"

"Hoot."

"I am Chipmunk. Who are you?"

"Hoot."

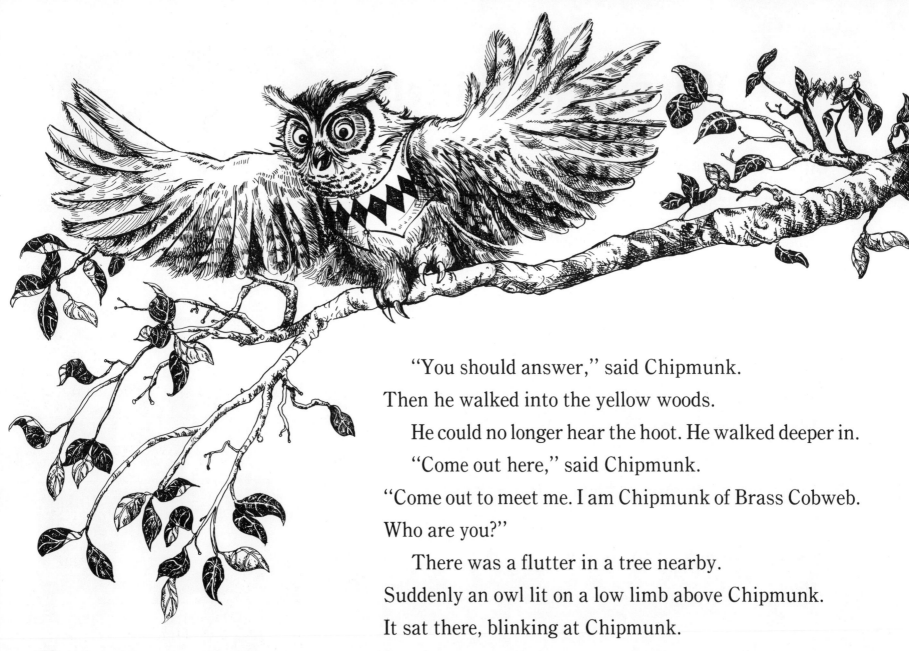

"You should answer," said Chipmunk.

Then he walked into the yellow woods.

He could no longer hear the hoot. He walked deeper in.

"Come out here," said Chipmunk.

"Come out to meet me. I am Chipmunk of Brass Cobweb.
Who are you?"

There was a flutter in a tree nearby.

Suddenly an owl lit on a low limb above Chipmunk.

It sat there, blinking at Chipmunk.

Chipmunk said, "I am Chipmunk.

I have set out to find a king for Brass Cobweb.

Who are you?"

"Hoot."

"Now—" Chipmunk said.

"No," said the owl. "I *am* Hoot. That is my name.

Where is Brass Cobweb?"

"It is five days down the road," said Chipmunk.

"Will you go far?" asked Hoot.

"As far as I must," said Chipmunk.

"I will come with you," said Hoot.

"I've never been on a trip."

"Come on then," said Chipmunk.

Hoot and Chipmunk left the yellow woods.

They went back to the road,

Hoot flying near the ground and Chipmunk walking.

Near night they stopped in an open field.

13

"Shall we sleep here?" asked Chipmunk.

"It's not wise," said Hoot. "I think we should find some cover. What if it rains? What if there are robbers?"

Chipmunk thought to himself, "Hoot has a good answer. He is wise."

At the edge of the field they found a good tree. It had thick branches for Hoot. It had a snug hole for Chipmunk. They took their places and fell asleep.

Crack!

Chipmunk sprang up.

Crack!

Hoot woke up.

Crack!

"What is it?" said Hoot in a whisper.

There was a very loud crack almost next to the tree they were in.

"Who is there?" Chipmunk called out.

Then in the dim moonlight Chipmunk could see
a big lizard hitting trees with a stick.
The lizard went from tree to tree.
He drew back his stick and *crack!* hit a tree.

Then the lizard came to the tree where
Hoot and Chipmunk were. He drew back his stick.

"Hoot!" said Hoot.

"Aha!" said the lizard. "There *are* beggars
in my woods. Come here. Let me see you!"

Chipmunk came out. Lizard lit a torch.

"Aha!" said Lizard again.
"Who are you? Why are you in my woods?"

"I am Chipmunk from Brass Cobweb.
I'm looking for a king."

"I am king here," said Lizard.
"And I am going to put you in jail."

"Me?" said Chipmunk. "Why?"

"You're on my land," said Lizard.

"I'll get off your land," said Chipmunk.

"Too late," said Lizard. "You broke the law."

"How could I know the law here?" asked Chipmunk.

From high in the tree Hoot said, "Hoot!"

"Who is up there?" asked Lizard.

"Hoot!" said Hoot.

"Answer me!" Lizard yelled.

"He did," said Chipmunk. "His name is Hoot."

"Come here, Hoot," said Lizard. "Let me see you."

Hoot flew to a lower branch.

The light from the torch made his gray feathers yellow.

"You are going to jail too," said Lizard.

"Why?" asked Hoot.

"You are on my land," said Lizard.

"You broke the law."

Hoot said, "Tell me just what your law says."

"It says that no one may be on my land," said Lizard. "I say who will be on my land."

"Is that just what the law says?" asked Hoot.

"Yes!" yelled Lizard.

"Then you can't put me in jail," said Hoot.

"What?" said Lizard. "Why not?"

"I haven't been on your land. I'm not on your land now. I'm in a tree," said Hoot.

"The trees are mine too," said Lizard.

"The law doesn't say so," said Hoot. "Come up here, Chipmunk."

Before Lizard could stop him, Chipmunk scrambled up the tree trunk and out on the limb to Hoot.

"Get on my back," said Hoot.

Chipmunk climbed onto Hoot. He sat between his wings.

"Now," said Hoot to Lizard,
"let's talk about my friend, Chipmunk."

Lizard started to climb the tree.

"Do not come up here," said Hoot. "I'll fly away."

Lizard got down again.

"What about Chipmunk?" he asked.

"Where was Chipmunk
when you found him?" asked Hoot.

"In this hole," said Lizard.

"And where is the hole?" asked Hoot.

"The hole is in the tree," said Lizard.

"So it is," said Hoot. "You can't put
Chipmunk in jail. He wasn't on your land."

"Yes, he was," said Lizard.
"He was on my land just now."

"But," said Hoot, "you told him to be there.
The law says that you will say
who's to be on your land."

"Wait!" said Lizard. "Chipmunk can't fly.
He must have been on my land to get to the tree!"

"Did you see him?" asked Hoot.

"No," said Lizard.

"Do you see any tracks?" asked Hoot.

"No," said Lizard.

"Can you prove
that Chipmunk was on your land?" asked Hoot.

"No," said Lizard.

"Then you cannot put Chipmunk in jail.
You cannot put me in jail. We are not on your land."

"Fiddlesticks!" said Lizard. "You're too smart for me.
You and Chipmunk can sleep here tonight."

"Thank you," said Chipmunk.

He started to climb down. Hoot stopped him.

"Thank you, Lizard," said Hoot.
"But we must be going."

With that he spread his wings
and flew off into the night with Chipmunk.

"Thank you for your help," said Chipmunk.
"You could have left me.
Lizard couldn't have caught you."
He pulled his shell hat down on his ears.

"You're my friend," said Hoot.

"You are true and wise," said Chipmunk.
He began to think that Hoot might make a good king.

"I will fly all night," said Hoot.
"I am used to it. I like to sleep in the day."

"But I like to sleep at night," said Chipmunk.
"I need to look for a king by day."

"It's not safe to sleep at night," said Hoot.
"It's better to sleep in the daytime."

"I always sleep at night," said Chipmunk.

"I don't," said Hoot. "I watch at night.
I watch for rain. I watch for robbers."

Chipmunk thought a while.

Then he said, "Are you afraid, Hoot?"

Hoot did not answer. He just flew on.
His big wings flapped loudly.

Chipmunk said, "Is that why
you wouldn't stay in the tree? Were you afraid of Lizard?"

Hoot said, "I didn't trust him.
He might have robbed us."

Chipmunk said, "All I have
is a bundle of nuts and corn. Oh no!"

"What?" said Hoot.

"I left my bundle in the tree!
Let's go back and get it!"

"No," said Hoot. "It's not safe."

Chipmunk said, "Lizard is not bad. Lizard was going
by the law. He did not want to rob us. Let's go back."

"You cannot be sure," said Hoot.
"We had better go on."

"But now I'll have no breakfast," said Chipmunk.

"I'll find you some," said Hoot.

Far away there was a low rumble.

"What was that?" said Hoot.

"Just thunder," said Chipmunk.

"Thunder far ahead."

Then a bolt of lightning lit the sky.

"A storm is coming!" said Hoot.

"We must go back to my yellow woods!"

"No," said Chipmunk. "Just land."

"No," said Hoot. "I am afraid of rain. I must go home!"

Hoot turned in the air so suddenly
that Chipmunk fell off.

"Help!" he cried. "Help!"

But Hoot only heard the thunder.

His fear got the best of him.

He flew toward his yellow woods.

The Seeds of Greed

3

Chipmunk fell and fell.

Then he landed on something warm and soft.

He bounced once and landed lightly again.

"Hey!" said the warm, soft thing.

"Who are you? What are you doing?"

"I beg your pardon," said Chipmunk.

"I am Chipmunk from Brass Cobweb. I fell off an owl!"

"Well! Why not get off me and let me see you?"

"Yes, yes," said Chipmunk.

He climbed down, holding on to thick fur.

He felt along a long body, then a neck, then a head.

At last he felt a cold, hard nose.

"Pardon me," said Chipmunk. "Ah, who are *you*?"

"Fox."

"Oh."

Fox blew on the coals of his fire. The fire flared up. His white teeth gleamed in the light.

"Well," said Fox. "You woke me up, Chipmunk."

"I beg your pardon. I'll be going now. You can go back to sleep."

"No, no," said Fox. "It's almost time to get up. Stay for breakfast."

Chipmunk said, "Do you want me to eat breakfast or *be* breakfast?"

Fox laughed. "Ho, ho, Chipmunk. I do not eat chipmunks. I eat what you eat. What do you eat?"

"I eat nuts and corn," said Chipmunk.

"Good," said Fox. "As soon as it gets light we will have breakfast. Sit down, Friend. Rest."

Chipmunk sat down. It began to get light.

Fox and Chipmunk ate nuts for breakfast. Chipmunk noticed that Fox had a hard time cracking the shells.

"What is this place?" asked Chipmunk.

"Thunder Ridge," said Fox.

"Why is it called that?" asked Chipmunk.

"It thunders here every night," said Fox.

"Does it rain too?" asked Chipmunk.

"No. It just thunders. Tell me about Brass Cobweb. Why is it called that?" said Fox.

Chipmunk thought of his home. He felt sad. He wanted to see his friends. But he had not yet found a king.

"The gate is a big brass cobweb."

"How did that get there?" asked Fox.

"No one knows. Not even Grandmother Cricket can say. It is very old."

"What are you doing here?" asked Fox.

Chipmunk did not quite like the look Fox gave him. He thought of the white teeth.

Chipmunk said, "I'm on a trip.
But the owl who was with me went home.
He's afraid of rain. The thunder scared him."

"I see," said Fox. "Will you go home too?"

"No," said Chipmunk. "I'll go on."

"Well," said Fox. "I like to take trips.
I'll go with you. I'll pack a sack."

So Chipmunk and Fox set off that day,
Fox walking slowly and Chipmunk walking fast.

They saw a field of flowers a mile wide. Every flower
was a different color, but they all smelled like cinnamon.

One day they found some stones in a cave.
The stones had sharp prickles all over like burrs have.
A rabbit there said the stones were seeds. He said they
grew into hills overnight. Fox put some into his sack.

They came to a valley of yellow trees and
hummingbirds and corn.

"Look!" said Fox. "Corn! Let's have a big breakfast!"

"We must pay for this. It's not ours!" said Chipmunk.

"We'll pay," said Fox. "We'll pay."

Fox reached out for an ear of corn. Suddenly
a grapevine wrapped around him. Chipmunk
sprang up to help. But a big net flopped down on him.

"Hey!" said Chipmunk.

A band of raccoons jumped out of hiding.
They made a ring around Fox and Chipmunk.

"So," said the biggest raccoon.
"Here are the thieves. Tie them up!"

In a flash, Chipmunk and Fox sat tied to a tree.
The big raccoon stood in front of them.
He tapped the sacks that Fox and Chipmunk had carried.

"What's in here? My corn?" he asked.

"No!" said Chipmunk. "Our breakfast is in there. We brought it with us."

"Let's see," said the big raccoon. He bent over to open a sack.

"Wait!" said Fox.

The raccoon jerked up. He looked at Fox. "Do you have something to hide, Fox?"

"Not at all," said Fox. "I just don't want you to get hurt."

"How would I get hurt?" said the raccoon. "What do you have in here?"

"There are some nuts. There is the corn we brought with us. And there are some seeds," said Fox. "Don't touch the seeds."

"What kind of seeds?" asked the raccoon.

"Hard, prickly seeds," said Fox.

"Seeds for what?" said the raccoon.

Fox said, "Never mind. Just don't plant them."

Chipmunk thought, "Fox is clever. He is brave too. He tries a trick when he is tied to a tree."

The raccoon called for his friends. He told them about the seeds.

"What do you think?" said the big raccoon. "What do you think they grow?"

No one could say.

"Tell us what seeds you have," said the biggest raccoon to Fox. "Tell us."

Fox shook his head.

One small raccoon said, "It must be some wonderful food. That's why Fox won't say."

Another raccoon said, "Let's plant some and see what grows."

"No!" Fox said. "Don't do that!"

The raccoons opened the sack.
They took out the seeds.

Fox said, "Don't plant them all.
At least leave me one."

"Oh no," said one raccoon. "We'll teach you not to be greedy. You stole our corn. We'll plant your seeds."

And so they did. They planted a whole row of seeds. They planted them right in front of Fox and Chipmunk. They watered the seeds.

"Now we'll see," said Big Raccoon.

"Yes," said Fox. "Now we'll see."

The raccoons had a big feast of corn. They ate and ate. At last they went to sleep. Chipmunk tried to stay awake. But he was tired. He had walked all day. He fell asleep.

Near morning he heard a loud roar.
He started to get up, but the grapevine rope still held him.

"Fox!" he said.

"It's working!" said Fox. "Get ready!"

Underground the seeds were getting bigger and bigger. They pushed up the dirt. They pushed up more dirt. Suddenly a row of hills rose up. The hills came up right in front of Fox and Chipmunk.

Then the tree began to tip over. As the hills grew, the tree tipped more.

"We're going to fall!" said Chipmunk.

"Here's our chance!" said Fox. "The tree will fall over. We'll slip the rope off. We'll run!"

Suddenly the tree fell over. The branches cracked. The roots stuck up.

"Now," said Fox. "Wiggle down out of the ropes."

Fox was strong. He wiggled out of the rope.

"Help!" said Chipmunk. "Help me!"

From the top of the new hill came a shout. The band of raccoons was coming.

"Help!" said Chipmunk.

"Too late!" said Fox. "They see us."

"Wait!" said Chipmunk.

"No," said Fox over his shoulder. "I won't get caught again." And, running away, he laughed.

"You are no true friend," said Chipmunk. "I would help *you!*"

But Fox was already gone.

Chipmunk very much missed his home right then. He wished he were sitting by Glass Pond with Rat, and Crab, and Ant, and Bass, and Grandmother Cricket.

"Where's your friend?" asked Big Raccoon.

"He's not my friend," said Chipmunk.

"Well, where is Fox?" said Big Raccoon.

"I don't know," said Chipmunk. "He's gone."

"We still have you," said Big Raccoon.

"But I didn't steal your corn. I didn't try to.
I am Chipmunk from Brass Cobweb.
I am looking for a king. Please let me go."

Big Raccoon said, "Perhaps you didn't steal our corn.
But you ruined our field with these hills!"

Chipmunk said, "*You* planted the seeds.
You watered them. *You* ruined your own field!"

"He's right," said another raccoon.

"Yes," said another, "you ruined our field!"

"What?" said Big Raccoon. "How dare you say that?
You helped me plant the seeds. You helped me water
them. You ruined our field. It wasn't I. It was you!"

An old raccoon said, "No, it was you!"

Big Raccoon said, "It was you."

Another said, "It was Big Raccoon.
He shouldn't be leader. Big Raccoon is a bad leader!"

And then a fight started. The raccoons pounced
on each other. They boxed each other's ears.
They tore up stalks of corn to fight with.
They yelled. They growled.

Chipmunk wiggled and wiggled. Chipmunk finally
wiggled out of the rope. He climbed down the root.
No one saw him. All the raccoons were fighting.
Chipmunk jumped off the roots. He ran up the hill.
He ran and ran. He was far away by night.

Daring in the Dunes

Chipmunk sat by a small lake.
The water lapped the shore.
He thought of Mint Lake and Glass Pond.
He wanted to go home.

"I can't go home," he said aloud.
"I haven't found a king."

"What's that you say?" said someone in the water.
"Who wants to go home?"

"I'm Chipmunk from Brass Cobweb. Who are you?"

"I am Squire Turtle. I live here in Wonder Lake.
You can live here. This can be your home."

Chipmunk said, "You're kind.
But I miss my old friends."

"Yes," said Turtle. "It's good to have friends.
Who are your friends?"

Chipmunk said, "There is Rat. He's the banker. Ant is a storekeeper. There are Bass and Crab. And there is Grandmother Cricket. She's old and wise. I would like to talk to her right now."

Turtle said, "You must be a good chipmunk. You have many friends. I'll be your friend too."

"Thank you," said Chipmunk. "Tell me, Friend, why is this called Wonder Lake?"

Turtle swam over. He climbed out and sat on the bank with Chipmunk.

Said Turtle, "The lake changes temperatures. Sometimes it is warm. Sometimes it is cold. Sometimes it is hot. Sometimes it is just right. We always wonder what temperature it will be next."

Chipmunk chuckled.

"That's a good reason," said he.

Turtle said, "Now you're not so sad. Tell me now why you can't go home."

"I must find a king for Brass Cobweb," said Chipmunk. "I have looked and looked. I must find a king who is brave and wise and true."

"How far will you go to find a king?" asked Turtle.

"I'll go to Seven Copper Hills," said Chipmunk. "Or as far as a month will take me."

"Well," said Turtle, "you're not far from Seven Copper Hills. In the morning I'll show you."

Chipmunk was glad. "Thank you," he said. "Thank you very much."

"Would you like some clover?" asked Turtle. "You can share my supper."

Chipmunk did not like clover. But he ate some and said thank you. He told Turtle about Hoot and Lizard. He told him about Fox and the raccoons.

"I got away," he said at last, "while the raccoons were fighting. I ran until I came to this lake. Then I met you."

Chipmunk felt sleepy. He yawned.

"Those are good stories," said Turtle. "You tell good stories. Sleep now. You're tired."

Chipmunk would have said thank you, but he fell asleep.

The next day Chipmunk and Turtle set out for Seven Copper Hills. Chipmunk looked for his shell hat.

"I must have lost my hat," he said. "I must have lost it when the tree fell over."

Turtle said, "Was it your best hat?"

"It was my only hat," said Chipmunk. "Oh, well. I will get another one some day."

Chipmunk rode on Turtle to the other side
of Wonder Lake. Today the water was cold.
It looked purple in the early morning light.

Chipmunk said, "We have purple grass
in the Dale of Snails."

Turtle said, "Is that a place in Brass Cobweb?"

"Yes," said Chipmunk.

"Purple grass," said Turtle. "How strange."

"I've seen many strange things," said Chipmunk.

He thought Wonder Lake was strange,

but he did not say so.

At the far shore, Chipmunk got off and walked.

Chipmunk walked slowly because Turtle walked slowly.

By noon, they could see Seven Copper Hills ahead.

The hills gleamed in the sun.

They made Chipmunk think of the gate at home.

"Who lives in Seven Copper Hills?" asked Chipmunk.

Turtle had to stop. He had to catch his breath
to speak. Walking is hard work for turtles.

"Puff," said Turtle. "Only Snake. Puff. And Gopher.
Puff. Puff. They are enemies to each other."

Turtle and Chipmunk walked on. It took two more
days to get to Seven Copper Hills. Chipmunk could have
made it in one day. But he did not like to leave Turtle.

"Here we are," said Turtle at last.
"The first of the Seven Copper Hills."

"It is beautiful here," said Chipmunk.
The sunset made the hills glow bright orange red.
The wide river looked like a strip of bronze.
Suddenly there was a splash in the center of the river.

"What was that?" said Chipmunk.

"That was just Old Trout," said Turtle. "He doesn't
care for company. He likes to have the river to himself."

Chipmunk and Turtle started on. From far ahead
there came a low rumble. It got louder.
It turned into a roar.

"Dust storm!" said Turtle. He began to dig a hole.
"Help me dig!"

Chipmunk and Turtle dug a small hole.
The roar was almost upon them.

"Get into the hole," said Turtle.

Chipmunk jumped in. Turtle lay across the top.
His shell was like a lid for the hole.
He pulled his head and legs inside the shell.

The dust storm rushed over Chipmunk and Turtle.
The wind roared. Sand whirled past. It got very hot.
Then the storm stopped. Everything was still.

Turtle got up and looked around. "It's over," he said.
"Come out and see."

Chipmunk scrambled out.
Everything looked changed.

"Are we in the same place?" Chipmunk asked. "Where is the river?"

"We are in the same place. The new dunes make it look like a new place. I think the river is just over that dune," said Turtle.

"Thank you for helping me," said Chipmunk. "You're a true friend."

Turtle said, "You're quite welcome. Friends help friends."

Chipmunk thought, "Turtle is brave too. Maybe Turtle would be a good king."

There were dunes on every side.

"Let's try to get out," said Chipmunk. "You lead the way."

Turtle climbed up a dune. Chipmunk went after him. But when they got to the top, they did not see the river.

"Oh my," said Turtle. "I think that we are lost."

Through the sand came Snake. He came through the dunes. He came slowly up to Turtle.

"Hiss," he said, "Are you lossst?" His eyes were slits. His tongue flicked in and out.

"I think we are," said Turtle. "Can you tell us the way to the river?"

"Yesss," said Snake. "Hiss. It'sss thisss way. Come with me. Hiss." He smiled a thin smile.

Turtle started to go down with Snake.

"Wait," Chipmunk whispered. "I don't trust Snake. Let's ask some more questions."

"No," said Turtle. "Snake wants to help. Let's go."

Chipmunk said, "Is Snake your friend? He is an enemy of Gopher."

"Everyone is *my* friend," said Turtle.

Chipmunk did not like the look Snake gave him.
It made him think of Fox.

"I'll stay here," Chipmunk said.

"I'll come back for you," said Turtle.

Turtle went off with Snake.

Chipmunk watched them go. Then he sat down to think.
He said to himself, "There are the Seven Copper Hills.
If the hills are still in the same place,
the river must be over there. Yes, I think it is.
Oh dear, that's not the way Snake and Turtle went."

Chipmunk thought it over. He could go to the river
and start for home. He could go after Turtle.
At last he stood up and sighed. He went after Turtle.

Late that night, Chipmunk saw a fire. It was Snake's
fire. Chipmunk got close. He saw Turtle in a cage.

Chipmunk thought, "Turtle is brave,
and Turtle is true. But Turtle isn't wise. I must help him."

"Hey, Snake!" Chipmunk called from his hiding place. "Lazy Snake!"

"Who isss there?" hissed Snake. "Isss that you, Gopher?"

"What if it is? What will you do? You cannot catch me in the dark, Slow Bones!" said Chipmunk.

"Come out here where I can sssee you and sssay that! Hiss!" said Snake.

"Oh no," said Chipmunk. "You come up here. Or are you afraid of me?"

"Ssso!" hissed Snake. "We'll sssee who isss afraid of who!"

Snake shot out toward Chipmunk. Chipmunk ran to a new spot. He waited for Snake to say something.

"Now who'sss afraid?" hissed Snake.

"Not me," said Chipmunk. Then he ran to a new place.

Far into the night, Chipmunk played his game. At last Snake wore out. He fell asleep far from his fire.

Chipmunk ran back to Turtle. He opened the cage. Turtle climbed out.

"Come with me to the river. It's not far," Chipmunk said.

When morning came, Chipmunk and Turtle were far
down the river. The river flowed into Wonder Lake.
Today the lake was warm.

"Home again," said Turtle.

Chipmunk said, "It's time I started for home myself."

Said Turtle, "Thank you for helping me.
I shouldn't have trusted Snake."

Chipmunk said, "You helped me. I helped you.
Friends help friends."

Turtle went up on the shore. Chipmunk got off.
They went to look for supper.
This time Chipmunk had nuts.
Chipmunk and Turtle both said good-night and slept.

The Homecoming

5

Before light, Chipmunk was on his way.

He was a little sad.

He had not yet found a good king.

He was a little glad.

He wanted to go home, and now he was on his way.

He didn't go home the way he had come.

He looked and looked for someone to be king.

He looked in valleys. He looked in woods. He looked along rivers. He looked in fields. He looked beside ponds. But he didn't see a king for Brass Cobweb.

One day he began to see things he knew. It began to look like home. Then, all of a sudden, there stood the shining gate of Brass Cobweb.

"Oh," said Chipmunk. "I'm home! I'm home!"

He ran through the gate.

He ran past the Dale of Snails. He ran to Glass Pond. He stopped at the top of the bank. Below sat Rat and Ant and Crab and Grandmother Cricket. In the pond was Bass.

Chipmunk was so glad to see them that he almost cried. Then he remembered that he had not brought a king. He walked slowly down to his friends.

Bass saw him first.

"Chipmunk is home!" Bass said.

They all jumped up to meet him.

"Chipmunk, look at you!" said Ant. "Where is your hat? Where is your sack?"

"I lost them," he said.

"Chipmunk," said Crab. "You're very dusty. Where have you been?"

Rat said, "Did you find us a king?"

Chipmunk shook his head. "I'm sorry," he said. "I didn't find a king."

"Oh," said Bass.

"Oh," said Crab.

"Oh," said Ant.

"That's too bad," said Rat. "We've built him a fine house in Cricket Thicket."

"Yes," said Ant. "And we've made him a wonderful crown."

Chipmunk looked very sad. "I tried," he said. "But I couldn't find anyone who was brave and wise and true."

Grandmother Cricket said, "Tell us of your trip. What strange things did you see?"

She sat down. "Click. You must have many things to tell."

Chipmunk told them about Hoot. He told them about Lizard.

"Hoot," he said, "was wise and true. But Hoot was not brave."

"You flew with Hoot?" asked Ant.

"Yes," said Chipmunk.

"That was brave of you,"
said Grandmother Cricket. "Click."

"Do you think so?" he asked.

"What did you learn from Hoot?"
asked Grandmother Cricket.

"I learned that to be really wise, you must be brave,"
said Chipmunk.

"What did you learn from Lizard?" she asked.

"I learned that laws must be clear," Chipmunk said.

"What happened then?" said Bass.

"I fell off Hoot. I landed on a fox," said Chipmunk.
"He had big, white teeth."

Chipmunk told them about Fox. He told them about
the raccoons. He told them about the seeds and about
how he got away.

"Fox was brave and wise. But Fox was not true,"
he said.

"What did you learn from Fox?"
asked Grandmother Cricket.

"I learned that to really be brave you must be true,"
said Chipmunk. "I did not trust Fox.
He did not look true."

"That was wise of you," said Grandmother Cricket.

"What did you learn from the raccoons?" said Crab.

"I learned that greed is bad in a leader,"
said Chipmunk.

"What happened then?" said Bass.

Chipmunk told them about Turtle. He told them
about Snake. He told them about the dust storm.

"Turtle was brave, and Turtle was true.
But Turtle was not wise," said Chipmunk.

"What did you learn from Turtle?" asked Rat.

"I learned that to really be true, you must be wise,"
said Chipmunk. "I learned why Grandmother Cricket
said a good king must be all three things.
He must be brave *and* wise *and* true."

"What happened to Turtle?" asked Crab. "Did he get away?"

"I went back for him. I wore Snake out with a trick. Then Turtle and I went down the river."

"That was true of you," said Grandmother Cricket.

"What did you learn from Snake?" asked Ant.

"I learned that one who tries to trick can be tricked," said Chipmunk.

Grandmother Cricket said, "Click. You have brought us many good stories."

"But I did not bring a king," said Chipmunk. He looked down.

"Yes, you did," said Grandmother Cricket. "You brought us a king who is brave and wise and true."

"Who is it?" said Chipmunk.

"*You* are the king for Brass Cobweb," said Grandmother Cricket.

"Yes," said Rat, Bass, Ant, and Crab.

"I am?" asked Chipmunk, blinking.

"Yes," said Grandmother Cricket. "Click.
Bring the crown." She tapped her pine-needle cane.

They crowned Chipmunk that very day.
He went to live in the fine house in Cricket Thicket.
He had plenty of nuts and corn to eat.

King Chipmunk did not tax the kingdom. In fact,
he ran his mill on Windmill Hill the same as ever.
He sat by Glass Pond and told stories.
He almost forgot he was a king.
But he did brave deeds and gave wise answers
and was true to his friends.

And when anyone hears of Brass Cobweb now,
he does not hear about the cobweb gate.
He hears about the wise, true, brave king there.
He hears of King Chipmunk.

Publisher's Note

One of the most powerful tools in the world is a story. It can gain a heart that is cold to other approaches; it can teach without alienating; it can stay with the reader long after the book is closed, often revealing more about life as the reader's real experience broadens. All these things a story can do—and entertain at the same time.

A King for Brass Cobweb is a fable, a story that teaches lessons for people through animal characters. Like other fables, it presents character types: the wise and the naive, the noble and the selfish, the prudent and the rash. And while every reader, even the youngest, knows that animals never talk or elect kings, he may recognize in the animals certain qualities he has seen in himself or in others.

It is this identification with the characters that makes the fable important. When the reader sees some qualities praised and rewarded and other qualities condemned and punished, he may take stock of himself. He may finish the story wanting to nurture the good qualities he has seen and to rid himself of the faults. And because the fable operates in fantasy, the reader is free to make his evaluations indirectly and, therefore, more comfortably.

A King for Brass Cobweb is a fable that uses the genre's subtle persuasiveness for good. It praises the ability to stick to one's obligations despite personal discomfort; it shows the sad end of greediness and the shame of cowardice; it rewards not appearance or mere talent, but rather humility and readiness to learn. The young reader may well absorb these lessons all the while engrossed in a tale of a band of animals in search of a king.

Books by Dawn L. Watkins

Medallion
Jenny Wren
The Cranky Blue Crab
A King for Brass Cobweb